COUNT DRACULA

COUNT DRACULA

Abraham "Bram" Stoker

An imprint of Om Books International

First published in 2015

An imprint of Om Books International

Corporate & Editorial Office
A-12, Sector 64, Noida 201 301
Uttar Pradesh, India
Phone: +91 120 477 4100
Email: editorial@ombooks.com
Website: www.ombooksinternational.com

Sales Office
107, Darya Ganj,
New Delhi 110 002, India
Phone: +91 11 2326 3363, 2326 5303, 4000 9000
Fax: +91 11 2327 8091
Email: sales@ombooks.com
Website: www.ombooks.com

Illustrated by Manish Singh, Manoj Kumar Prasad

ISBN: 978-93-85031-53-3

Printed in India

10 9 8 7 6 5 4 3 2 1

Contents

Chapter One

The Strange Ride

Jonathan Harker's Journal

3 May, Bistritz

I took the train from Munich on the 1st, travelling to Transylvania. The little German I understand and speak, came in handy to get along with fellow passengers and stewards. I also read up about Transylvania; I felt it would impress the nobleman, Count Dracula, with whom I have business. I am a lawyer working in London. I have been sent by my company to show the Count several properties in London, which he had shown interest in purchasing.

During the journey, I had an excellent chicken basted in paprika, a porridge of maize flour that the locals call 'mamaliga', and a stuffed eggplant. The chicken was rather fiery for my taste and I longed for a sip of water all night.

Outside, there was beauty all around me. Sometimes we came across little towns or castles on the top of steep hills; sometimes we passed by rivers and streams. Cattle grazed peacefully on lush meadows.

It was late when we reached Bistritz, the town named by the Count. It was on the borders of three states: Transylvania, Moldavia and Bukovina. Count Dracula was known to be a descendant of Attila and the Huns. At the hotel, I received a letter from the Count:

> My friend,
>
> Welcome to the Carpathians.
>
> The landlady will help you with the carriage for your travel from there.

I hope your trip was a happy one and that you will enjoy your stay in my beautiful land.

Dracula

The hotel was pleasant enough and I tried to fall asleep, but cannot, which is strange.

5 May

Just before I was leaving, the old landlady came up to my room and said in a hysterical tone, "Do you haf to go? Oh! Young man, do you haf to go?" She was so excited that she was mixing languages I did not understand at all. She let me go only after I agreed to wear the crucifix she offered to keep me safe. I found this behaviour very strange, indeed.

Outside, the carriage driver appeared to be a strange man. Many townspeople had gathered around my carriage and they all looked worried.

Many of them crossed themselves. They seemed to have come to bid me goodbye. I found this behaviour strangely touching.

Were they so worried about me because I was a foreigner? Was it part of their hospitality?

I will never forget the sight of this motley group of farmers and peasants, clinging to each other, reluctant to let me go. The driver was tall and bearded, and seemed to be hiding behind a large hat.

As he spoke with the landlady, the light from the lamp fell on his hard face, with very red lips and sharp-looking teeth as white as ivory. I thought this was a truly peculiar face and wondered if it had anything to do with the genetic disposition of the land. The landlady avoided looking into his eyes and was happy when he left her side.

He came towards me, put a thick, black cloak over my shoulders and handed me a pair of gloves. He said in excellent German, "The night is cold, dear sir, and my master, the Count, has asked me to take good care of you."

When the horses started pulling the carriage away, the old landlady gave me one last look, a little sigh and, once more, crossed herself.

As we rode along, the four small horses seemed to tremble. In the distance, the haunted howling of wolves could be heard. The driver patted and soothed the horses, and whispered something in their ears. Suddenly in the darkness, to my left, I saw a faint, flickering blue flame. The driver seemed to have seen it too.

At this point, he got off the carriage and walked into the darkness; at the same instant, the clouds parted to reveal the full moon.

In its light, I saw around us a ring of wolves, with white teeth and lolling red tongues. They had long, sinuous limbs and shaggy hair. I was stunned. My heart leapt. I realised I had absolutely no weapon against them and no means to disperse them. They started howling, as if the moon had a peculiar power over them.

The horses reared sharply in fright, their eyes rolling with a fear that sickened me to the core. Petrified, I did not move until the carriage driver returned. I desperately wished I could do something to make the wolves go away.

Out of the dark, from the forest, came the driver. He raised his voice commandingly and swept his long arms, as if sweeping aside some obstacle, and the wolves fell back.

Just then, a heavy cloud blocked out the moon, and when I could see again, the driver had climbed into the carriage and the wolves had disappeared.

All this filled me with dread. I was too scared to talk or even move.

We kept riding on, ascending and descending the rocky countryside. Suddenly, I realised that the driver was slowing down and I looked out.

Silhouetted against the full moon sky rose a vast, ruined castle. It had tall spires from whose tall, black windows came no ray of light and

whose broken battlements ran like a jagged line against the moonlit sky.

When the carriage stopped, the driver jumped down and held out his hand to help me down. His hand felt as strong as steel and I knew that he could crush me if he wanted to. He took my luggage and placed it on the ground and I stood next to the great door of the old castle, Castle Dracula, in the courtyard.

As I stood looking, the heavy stone door was unlocked. I could hear the bolts swinging back and the door opened with a slow, grating sound that got on my nerves.

Inside stood a tall, old man—clean shaven save for a long, white moustache. He held in his hand an antique silver lamp in which a flame burned, casting long, quivering shadows as it flickered in the draught coming through the open door. He was wearing all black clothes.

As he led me inside, he said, in excellent English, but with a slight East European accent,

"I am Dracula. Welcome to my house. Enter freely and of your own will."

There was a chill in the air. But I'm not sure that had anything to do with the chill running down my spine at his sight.

Count Dracula made no move or gesture to meet me, and stood like a statue, as though this little speech to welcome me had turned him into stone.

Chapter Two

Prisoner

Jonathan Harker's Journal (continued)

However, the instant I stepped over the threshold, he stepped forward, almost impulsively to receive me.

His firm handshake was similar to that of the carriage driver and for a moment I thought maybe they were the same person!

He took my bags from me. When I protested, he said, "No! No! Mr Harker, you are my guest. My people are not available at the moment. But it is my duty to ensure that you are comfortable. Also, you must be tired and need to eat and sleep. Please come this way."

He insisted on carrying my bags along the passage and then up a great, winding stair, and down another big passage. Our steps echoed heavily on the stone floor. At the end of this passage, he threw open a heavy door and I was happy to see a well-lit room in which a table was spread for supper, and on whose mighty hearth a great fire of logs – freshly replenished – flamed and flared. This didn't make me feel as out of place as I had been feeling so far.

The Count halted, putting down my bags. Then he closed the door, and crossing the room, opened another door. This led into a small octagonal room lit by a single lamp, and seemingly without a window of any sort. Passing through this, he opened yet another door, and motioned me to enter.

It was a welcome sight.

After a hearty dinner of roast chicken and wine, I took the opportunity to observe the Count at close quarters.

He had a very strong face with sharp features. His nose had a high bridge and peculiarly arched nostrils. He had a high, regal forehead with hair growing scantily a round the temples, but profusely elsewhere. His eyebrows were very thick – almost meeting over the nose – with hair that seemed to curl. The mouth, as far as I could see under the heavy moustache, was fixed and rather cruel-looking. He had peculiar sharp, white teeth that protruded over the lips, whose remarkable red colour shocked me. His ears were pale, and extremely pointed at the top; the chin was broad and strong, and the cheeks firm, though thin. He was an extremely pale man, as though he never ventured out in the sun.

Soon, I took the Count's leave and retired to my bedroom.

Jonathan Harker's Journal

7 May

For the last couple of days, the Count and I have talked about the estate that he was planning to buy in England with my help. It was an estate called Carfax, no doubt derived from *quatre face,* as the house is four-walled.

We also spoke about many things regarding our different countries and I found the Count to be very learned and knowlegeable.

I came to know that he loved London and the people of my country, England. This was the reason he wished to settle down there after a while. He told me many stories about his ancestors, as if they were actually living and breathing in this castle.

But I noticed that he never joined me for any meals nor did I see him during the day. He always made some excuse or the other to get out of eating with me. Sometimes, he said he had already eaten and at others, that he wasn't hungry at all! I also had the distinct feeling that there were no servants in the house even though the house seemed to be in perfect order.

He told me once, "Mr Harker, you may go to any room in the castle, but you should not go to the rooms where the doors are locked."

He paused and a smile came to his lips as he continued, "For your own safety, of course! You are not of this land. And there are many things that will surprise you."

8 May

Today, when I was shaving, I felt a hand on my shoulder and the Count's voice said to me, "Good morning!"

I was startled because I had not seen his reflection in the mirror. As I turned, my razor swung and, accidentally, I cut myself. I was quite shocked, the entire room was reflected in the mirror. *How was it possible that the Count could not be seen in the mirror?*

When the Count saw the blood, a monstrous anger flashed in his eyes and within a second, his hand suddenly grabbed my throat.

I was so startled at this action, I jerked my hand up. His hand must have touched the chain with the crucifix the landlady had made me wear in Bistritz, because instantly he became calm.

He snatched my mirror and said, "This wretched thing that has caused this pain. Who needs this thing? Only the vain."

Saying this, he took the mirror and flung it out of the window. It broke into a thousand pieces on the ground below. I was quite annoyed, for how was I to shave without it. But he left the room without a word.

Over the next few days, I explored the castle because I had nothing much to do. I found that the castle was built on a rock with three sides facing a steep drop. Surely, I would have been smashed to pieces if I had jumped from there.

As far as the eye could see, there was thick dense forest—the kind infested with hungry wolves—that I had travelled through. This was a fortress built to withstand any attack.

The views from the different windows are beautiful, but I found only a few unlocked doors. In fact, all the doors leading to the outside world were locked and it looked like you could only leave the castle from the windows!

The castle feels like a prison and I think I am a prisoner!

When this thought came to me, I roamed the castle in a hurry, trying every door and looking out of every window. I behaved like a rat does in a trap.

The more I thought about it, the surer I became that I couldn't talk to the Count about this.

The Count knew well enough that I am *his* prisoner!

Chapter Three

The Count Leaves for England

Jonathan Harker's Journal

15 May

Despite the Count's warnings, I explored the various rooms in the castle. There was nothing much for me to do and no company at all. Hence, it was only natural that I took to exploring the castle and admiring its fine furnishing, opulence and the spectacular views from its high windows.

I particularly liked the window facing the south side since it had a very peaceful view. I leaned out in the moonlight and I suddenly saw something moving a storey below me to the left.

I think it came from the window of the Count's own room. What I saw shocked me out of my wits.

Dark against the silver night, I saw the Count's head coming out of a window. Slowly, his whole body emerged from the window. Holding on to the gaps in the walls, the Count was descending the wall, face down like a lizard!

He seemed completely at ease traversing the walls, against gravity. His fingers and toes grasped the surface in a manner no human could. His form had a distinct grace to it. But my blood ran cold at this ghastly sight. I quickly stepped back from the window, unwilling and unable to watch anymore.

There were dangers surrounding me that I dare not even think of. I am a prisoner of fate, and of Count Dracula.

I quickly returned to my room, with my heart in my mouth. Needless to say, I slept fitfully.

1 June

Once more, I saw the Count go out in this lizard-like fashion. Now I know for certain that there is something very dangerous about this place, not just peculiar, as I had initially thought. I craned my neck to see more, but the Count disappeared into a hole or crevice in the walls. Since the Count was out, I took this chance to explore the castle further and maybe find keys to the doors.

After trying my luck for several hours in vain, I found one particularly heavy door closed, but not locked. I tried to push and shove against it, but it wouldn't budge. I tried with all my might, but I couldn't move it an inch. Dejected, I gave up. I was tired so I sat at a table in that room and started writing my journal. After sometime, perhaps due to sheer mental fatigue, I fell asleep.

When I woke up, I sensed the presence of someone else in the room. I did not want to immediately sit up as I didn't know what fresh hell awaited me. Instead, I slowly opened my eyes. In the moonlight, opposite me, I saw three young, very beautiful women. All three were uncommonly pale, had brilliant white, pointed teeth and dark red lips.

They said in a musical, haunting voice, "Oh! What do we have here?"

I kept my eyes closed and pretended to sleep. Though I am a married man and love my wife, Mina, ver much, I felt a strange attraction to these women. One of them came close to me and bent down close to me, and I could feel her teeth on my neck!

At that moment, the Count entered the room and pulled her angrily away from me. In a voice which was low, but still seemed to cut through the air, he whispered, "How dare you touch him? This man belongs to me!" He spoke like hellfire turned loose.

"Then do we have nothing tonight?" said one of the women.

The Count pointed to a sack in the corner which seemed to have something moving inside. The women jumped forward and opened the sack. It seemed a small, mewling baby was inside it! The women gleefully disappeared with the bag in an instant. All this was too much for me and I became unconscious.

When I woke up, I was back in my own bed. I tried going back to the room, where I remember the events had taken place, but I found it locked.

17 June

Today, I saw gypsies riding up to the castle with many large, square boxes, with handles of rope. I rushed to the door, but to my dismay, found that my room was locked. I tried to wave so I could gain their attention, but couldn't. But I could hear some work going on inside the castle.

18 June

I decided to search for the key again. I was sure it must be in the Count's room, but his room was locked.

In desperation, I risked my life and climbed down to the Count's room, by scaling the wall of the window just above.

I could not find the key, but found a staircase that led to the basement. There, I discovered the boxes that the gypsy people had brought with them. There were fifty boxes in all and in one of them lay the Count!

The Count looked younger. The moustache and the hair were a dark grey and there was fresh blood on his lips. His eyes were open and he was smiling cruelly—a smile so malicious it could have held its own in the deepest parts of Hell.

I ran back to my room when I heard one of the gypsies returning. After a few hours, I saw them leaving the castle with the fifty boxes. So, the Count had left the castle.

It seems to me that I am alone with the three ladies and I will be the dinner tonight.

Chapter Four

Dracula's First Strike

Mina Harker's Journal

24 July

Lucy met me at the station, looking sweeter and lovelier than ever. She was very eager to tell me about her engagement to Mr Arthur Holmwood. He is a wealthy and intelligent young man. She was very happy and excited about it. I am happy to be around familiar company for I miss my husband very much.

I still haven't received a letter from Jonathan after he left for his business trip to Transylvania. I hope he is well and thinking of me.

3 August

Lucy lives very close to the sea. I enjoy being here; London may be by the mighty Thames, but no open sea can be viewed from there. Oh! I do believe sea breeze is something else altogether.

Every day, we go sit on a bench overlooking the dock. It's a pleasant place to talk and take in the breeze.

But today was different. The wind was stronger. Grey clouds were swarming above us. The docked ships were having a hard enough time, let alone the ones that were trying to dock in the turbulent waters.

Today, we saw a strange ship in the horizon. An old man pointed at it and said to us, "That ship is not going in the right direction! The wind is strong, but it seems to be going against it somehow."

He paused, looking at the dark clouds behind the ship, and said, "You ladies better get home, there is a storm coming! Safer to be home!"

Cutting From *The Times*, 5 August

One of the greatest storms on record has just been experienced here today.

In the storm, a large ship was seen entering the dock. The ship swayed in the storm without direction, but seemed to be helped by the wind at every turn. It was a surprise to the people at the dock that the ship managed to get to the dock in one piece.

There was also a large black dog seen running away from the ship the moment it hit the dock.

When people got close to the ship, they were shocked to find that there was only one dead man on board, tied to the steering wheel with a crucifix! So how did the ship dock? Who steered it? Did it not have a crew to run it?

Many questions plagued the authorities, till the ship's logs were found.

The ship's logs told the story of a mysterious, tall, pale, old man seen wandering on the ship. One by one, the crew members disappeared and the last man, the Captain, tied himself to the steering wheel, for the remaining journey, with a crucifix.

The only luggage that the ship had was a delivery of fifty large boxes.

The crowd was in awe of the Captain's bravery and also of the miraculous way in which the ship reached the dock. More details to follow in the next issue.

Mina Harker's Journal
8 August

Lucy was restless all night. She went to the dock on her own, to sit on the bench in the moonlight. She said she needed the fresh air as it would do her good. I was reluctant to stay home without Lucy. After a while, I followed in her footsteps and joined her at the dock.

It is not a long walk to the dock. As I was nearing the bench, I had a clear view of Lucy silhoutted against the dark. But I thought, I saw a dark shape bending over Lucy on the bench.

At first, I thought it may be Arthur, but it seemed unlikely. I shouted out to her in fright, "Lucy! Lucy!" and hurried to the bench.

When I got there, Lucy was alone, but seemed to be sick. She was breathing heavily and was looking rather pale. So, I took her back home immediately. She was gasping for air, as if it was difficult for her to breathe. She looked weak and exhausted by the time I got her into bed for some rest.

After I had helped her into bed, I noticed two holes on the side of her neck. There was also a spot of blood on her blouse. I could not understand anything from this. *Had she been bitten by someone? Or something?*

If her condition doesn't improve in the morning, I will have to call a doctor.

9 August

Lucy looked well in the morning, so I decided against calling a doctor. We went to the dock again, to sit at the bench in the evening.

The sea breeze lifted Lucy's spirits and seemed to add some colour to her cheeks. We had been silent for a while when Lucy said, in a soft voice, "Those red eyes again! They are just the same."

She seemed to be looking at a tall, pale old man seated at another bench.

His eyes blazed red for an instant when I looked at him.

Chapter Five

Lucy's Condition Worsens

Dr John 'Jack' Seward's Journal
5 June

I have picked out a patient who is very interesting. I questioned him more throughly today than I have ever done, with a view to making myself a master of the facts relating to his mental illness.

R M Renfield: Strong, death excites him, moments of gloom, all towards some fixed idea, which I cannot make out. He is a peculiar sort of fellow. His good quality is his love of animals. But his pets are sort of odd, and many times he is cruel to them.

At the moment, his hobby is catching flies. The quantity of the flies in his room was so high that I had to tell him to stop. He threw a tantrum, but I refused to change my opinion. He thought about it and asked, "May I have three days?" I agreed to that.

I must watch him further. This case needs constant attention and observation.

18 June

Renfield is now fascinated with spiders, and has got many, very big fellows in a box. He has used his flies to catch the spiders!

19 July

He has moved on to sparrows, with the flies and spiders almost gone. I caught him feasting on them and relishing their blood! Most interesting. He asked for a kitten, which I refused.

19 August

I was in bed, when the flustered night watchman rushed to my room. He said that

Renfield had escaped. I ran to his room and the attendant pointed me in the direction he ran.

I saw Renfield just as he climbed over the high wall which separates our grounds from those of the deserted house to our left.

I got a ladder and dropped down to the other side. It was a dark night, but I was determined to find Renfield. On the far side of the house, I found him pressed close to the door of the church. I heard him say, "I am here at your service, Master. You will reward me, for I have been, and shall always be faithful. Now that you are near, I await your commands."

I was accompanied by the night watchman and two attendants. When we tried to hold him, he fought hard. He put in a Herculean effort to escape. But then a strange thing happened.

He doubled his efforts for an instant—his eyes wide and alarmed—and then suddenly grew calm. I followed his eye, but I could see nothing except a big bat. The bat was flapping away in a straight line unlike other bats I had seen. Renfield seemed to take instruction from it, as he nodded. He looked at the bat for a long time. I guessed it was his love for unusual creatures that calmed him down.

Letter: Arthur Holmwood to Dr Seward

My dear John,

I want you to do me a favour. Lucy, my betrothed, is rather ill, that is, she has something which cannot be described. She looks bad, feels very restless and is getting worse everyday. Some days she is too weak to walk about. I am sure there is something on her mind.

I have told her mother that I will ask you to check up on her.

My father's not well either and so I won't be there to see you. Send me a telegram, if necessary.

Thank you for your kindness, dear friend.

Arthur

Letter: Dr Seward to Arthur Holmwood

My dear Arthur,

I have seen Lucy, but can't put a finger on the problem. She complains of difficulty while breathing and of scary dreams. She was also somewhat bloodless, that is, her blood count seemed rather low and I had taken a sample to check it.

The blood analysis showed nothing out of the ordinary, but I am in doubt. I have written to my friend and master, Professor Abraham Van Helsing from Amsterdam, who knows as much about difficult diseases as anyone in the world. He will be coming over shortly to have a look at her.

I'll mail you of the progress.

Yours forever,

John Seward

Chapter Six

Jonathan Escapes

Mina Harker's Journal
19 August

Today, Lucy seemed to be in a talkative mood. I asked her if she had dreamed at all that night. She went on, in a dream-like state, as if trying to recall it herself.

"I don't know why, but this dream felt real. I was passing through the streets and over the bridge. A fish leaped as I went by and I leaned over to look at it. I kept looking, but couldn't find it. Then, I thought I saw something with red eyes, just like the man we saw. Terror filled me, Mina. My soul seemed to go out

from my body and floated in the air. Then, I felt you shaking my body and I came back."

All this sounded very bad to me. Finally, I have some news of Jonathan!

My dearest husband has been ill and that is why he hasn't written.

I am to leave in the morning and go over to Jonathan, and help to nurse him, if necessary, and bring him home.

I have packed my luggage for tomorrow and am all set to leave.

Letter: Mina Harker to Lucy
24 August, Budapest

My dearest Lucy,

I understand you are very anxious to know about all that has happened.

When I finally saw Jonathan, he looked pale, thin and weak. He has experienced something terrible and I fear it might be too much to ask him to recall it.

When he woke up, he asked me for his coat, as he wanted to get something from the pocket.

He took out his journal and then said to me, in a pained voice, wrought with fever, "Mina. You know, I believe there should be no secrets between husband and wife. I have gone through a terrible, terrible ordeal. I have feared for my life at every step. I don't know if I was dreaming or if my trouble was real. The doctors say I had brain fever by which they meant I was going mad. The secret is in this journal, but I don't want to know what is in it. I wrote in it when I thought I was lucid. But after the doctor's diagnosis, I have begun to doubt myself. I want to move on in life with happiness, just the way we imagined it would be before our marriage. So, I entrust you with this journal. Keep it safe. Read it, if you want to, but don't let me know what's in it unless it is very important to our future."

With that, he fell on the bed, exhausted.

I took the journal, wrapped it tight in a white paper and tied it with a pale blue ribbon. I used my wedding ring as a seal over the knot of the ribbon.

When Jonathan woke up again, I showed him what I had done and said that I was happy that he was back with me, and that I would only open the journal in case of grave danger. I didn't feel the need to revisit the reason behind his ill health, especially as he already seemed on the mend. He seemed very pleased and slept with my hands in his.

I will write again soon. Take care of your health.

Your ever-loving,

Mina Harker

Lucy Westenra's Journal

4 September

Mother wasn't too well. I couldn't quite make out what was wrong with her. I tried

to stay awake by her side, but I could hardly keep up. There seems to be a crazed bat at the window, scratching and flapping.

I don't really mind it, but it seems to be here every night.

I had more bad dreams. I wish I could remember them.

My face looks paler. I will try to cheer up when Arthur comes or he will be worried.

Letter: Dr Seward to Arthur Holmwood

My dear Art,

Professor Van Helsing has come and gone. He made a very careful examination of the patient, Lucy, and seemed very worried. His exact comment was, "It is a matter of life and death, perhaps even more!"

Don't worry about that, as he will speak plainly enough when the time comes. As he says, "Everything has a reason!"

John Seward

Lucy Westenra's Journal

5 September

There is something very wrong with me. I feel myself slipping out of my own grasp. I feel too exhausted to think straight. And how these nightmares trouble me every night!

I am ashamed to admit, but I must—I feel an unquenchable thirst for blood! Yes, blood! I feel so weak and an ache gnaws at my insides. I feel as if I am changing somehow. How I wish Arthur was by my side.

Chapter Seven

Lucy Needs Blood

Dr Seward's Journal

6 September

Lucy looked worse than before. I sent a telegram to Van Helsing to come at once.

When Van Helsing came, he looked shocked. His eyebrows converged till they almost touched over his nose. Lucy lay motionless and did not seem to have the strength to speak. Van Helsing followed me out of the room. He said hurriedly, "There is no time to be lost. She will die if she is not given blood. We need to have a blood transfusion as soon as possible."

I immediately said to him, "I am younger and stronger, Van Helsing. Let me be of help."

Van Helsing performed the blood transfusion, as soon as he could. And slowly, colour returned to Lucy's cheeks.

Afterwards, Van Helsing said to me, "I must return home to read from a few books about the two holes in her neck. You must remain here all night and not let her out of sight."

9 September

It has been three nights since I have been watching over Lucy. Her health seems to have returned, but she still looks a bit pale. I, myself, was tired from going to the hospital, working in the day and guarding Lucy at night.

Lucy saw me and said, "No sitting up for you tonight, Doctor. I am quite well."

She saw that I wouldn't listen to her, so she insisted, "Or else you can sleep in the room adjoining mine and I will keep the doors open,

so that if I need something, then I can call out to you."

This arrangement sounded fine to me and I agreed, reminding her to call me if she wanted something.

10 September

I woke up to see both Arthur and Van Helsing in the house. Arthur said, "I was extremely worried, so I came as quickly as I could. Father is feeling better now. So, this is Dr Van Helsing, I am grateful for your help, Sir!"

We entered Lucy's room to check on her. She seemed much worse than before.

Van Helsing quickly rubbed her palm, wrist and heart with some brandy. He said, "It is not too late! Her heart beats, but very weakly. We need to perform another transfusion as quickly as possible. Arthur, we will need your help."

"Anything you need, Sir. I will do anything for her."

Van Helsing performed the transfusion and Lucy seemed to be alive again.

Lucy slept all day and woke up fairly strong. Van Helsing went out to post a telegram and again asked me to watch over Lucy. When he returned, he told me that tonight he would stay with Lucy and asked me to go home and get some well-deserved rest.

11 September

I returned to Lucy's place in the afternoon. Shortly after I arrived, a big parcel came for the Van Helsing. He smiled and opened it to show a huge bouquet of white flowers.

"These are for you, Miss Lucy," he said.

"For me? Oh! Thank you!"

When she took the flowers, and smelled them, she smiled and said, "But these are only common garlic flowers."

Van Helsing said, "Yes, they are. It will do you good to smell the fragrance of this flower.

Tonight, you sleep with a garland of these flowers on your neck, I am certain that this will help you."

Van Helsing was so confident about the flowers that he decided that Lucy could sleep alone in her room today. He instructed her to keep the door and the windows closed. He also asked her to wear the garland on her neck throughout the night and not take it off under any circumstance.

I am worried that Van Helsing is getting overconfident, just like I was two nights ago.

Chapter Eight

Lucy's Mother Dies

Dr Seward's Journal
13 September

Van Helsing and I arrived at Lucy's place at eight. We came across Lucy's mother inside the house. And she said, "You will be glad to know that Lucy is better. She looks a lot healthier. She is still sleeping and I think we can let her sleep for a while longer."

Van Helsing was very happy. He rubbed his hands together in delight and said, "My treatment is working!"

To which, she replied naively, "I helped too, you know."

"What do you mean, Madam?" asked Van Helsing, he was a little confused at her statement.

"Well, I was worried about Lucy and went to check on her in the night. I found the room was stuffy with the smell of garlic and so I opened the window, and took out all the garlic flowers. The fresh air must have done her good," she smiled and made her way to the kitchen.

Then, for the first time in my life, I saw Van Helsing break down. He held his hands over his head in a sort of mute defeat. "God! God! God! What has she done!" he groaned.

Suddenly, he jumped to his feet and said, "Come, we must act. No matter how many Devils are at us, we must fight them!"

Once again, we found Lucy pale and white. This disheartened us all. How hard we had all tried to make her better. Again, Van Helsing performed the operation for the blood transfusion, but this time he gave Lucy his

blood. Again, some colour returned to Lucy's cheeks and her breathing became regular.

He went downstairs and told Lucy's mother that she must not remove anything from Lucy's room without asking him first, that the flowers were of medicinal value and breathing their scent was part of the cure for Lucy. Mrs Westenra mutely nodded her agreement.

He told me I can excuse myself and leave for the hospital, and that he will send me a telegram if he needs me. He added, in a most resolute tone, that he will be guarding Lucy tonight.

Article from *The TIMES*

Wolf Escapes Zoo And Returns The Next Day

18 September

Yesterday, the local zoo reported a missing wolf from its pack. The zoo's officials reported that it was seen to be heading north, up a hill, with remarkable pace, as if it was purposefully on its way somewhere.

The zookeeper doubted if it would leave the grounds, considering the zoo had been its habitat throughout its life. This particular wolf was born and reared in the zoo. Why would it escape? It certainly hadn't learnt to hunt and can't feed itself. So, a search was conducted on the grounds with no success.

Today, when our reporter was at the zoo to take notes, the wolf returned mysteriously with glass pieces stuck on its neck—as if it had got into some trouble.

So, that brought to an end this strange escapade at the zoo, which had spread fear on the streets yesterday.

Dr Seward's Journal

17 September

I was reading my books in my office, when Renfield charged in. He had a knife in his hand and moved purposefully around the table. Before I could react, he slashed my wrist,

which caused it to bleed profusel, and also his own. I quickly focused on tying up my wrist, as he dropped to his knees and started licking the blood. He kept repeating,

"The blood is the life! The blood is the life!"

When the attendants came in, he readily went along with them to his room without a fight. I thought this was the complete opposite behaviour to when we had caught him the first night.

I have lost a lot of blood and am tired. I need rest, rest, rest.

Thankfully, Van Helsing hasn't sent a telegram for me. I will sleep tonight.

Telegram: Van Helsing to Dr Seward
17 September

I have to leave to take care of some important work. Do not fail to be at Lucy's side tonight. Take care that the flowers are not taken out.

Dr Seward's Journal

18 September

The attendant came in the morning to tell me that he had found a telegram addressed to me in Renfield's pocket. It was from Professor Van Helsing.

I am in shock as I hurry to Lucy's house. A whole night lost and I know from experience what can happen in the night!

Lucy Westenra's Journal

17 September

This is an exact record of what took place tonight. I am keeping it in my pocket because I am dying of weakness and this had to be done, so someone may be alerted upon reading this note.

I went to bed as usual, taking care to keep the garland around my neck as Dr Van Helsing had directed, and soon fell asleep.

He had told me that Dr Seward would come by to watch over me in the evening, but he didn't come. I do not blame him; I quite understand the pressures of running a mental asylum.

I was woken up by the sound of flapping at the window and mother, who had come to check on me. She was worried about me and so she slept besides me.

As she lay near me, there was more flapping on the window followed by a wolf's long, harsh howl, right outside. I felt weak with fear and the calm that followed was deceptive.

After a few moments of quiet, my bedroom window was shattered by a wolf, which had stuck its head in. Mother woke up with a start, and in her shock she pulled apart the garland.

She cried out, "Good Lord!" and pointed at the wolf. A strange sound came out of her throat and she fell over, as if struck by lightning.

The room seemed to spin around and I kept my eyes fixed on the window. The wolf drew his

head back and a lot of dust blew in. I couldn't move my body, as if I was under a spell. My poor mother had died of shock, I suppose. Her body was on top of me and it had grown cold already. I passed out.

I regained consciousness in a while and went outside to call the servants. My heart sank when I saw what had happened. They all lay helpless on the floor, breathing heavily. They all seem to have been drugged.

I made my way to my room and held my dead mother. The air seems to be full of specks floating and circling. I could still hear the wolf howling outside.

I am beyond fear. I feel only sadness. My dear mother is gone. I feel weak. It is time that I go too. Goodbye Arthur, if I don't survive this night. God be with you and me.

Chapter Nine

Lucy Breathes Her Last?

Dr Seward's Journal
18 September

I drove at once to Lucy's place. I knocked and rang the bell, but no one came to the door. After a while, Van Helsing too reached the place. He was shocked to see me and said, "How is she? Are we too late? Did you not get my telegram?"

I quickly relayed the sequence of events from the night before. He paused and said solemnly, "Then I fear we are too late. God's will be done."

We went to the back of the house where we found a kitchen window open and I entered the house, and let Van Helsing in, from the front door. All the servants seemed to have been drugged and were breathing with difficulty. We immediately made our way to Lucy's room. With fear in our hearts, we pushed the door gently and opened the room.

On the bed lay two women, Lucy and her mother. Lucy's mother was covered in a white sheet, but her face was visible. A light breeze coming through a broken window must have blown the sheet off her face. Her face was white with a look of immense terror. By her side, lay Lucy whose face was paler than ever before. Without a word, Van Helsing bent over the bed to check on Lucy. He leapt to his feet at once and cried out, "It is not too late! Quick! Bring me the brandy!"

I flew downstairs and returned with the required bottle. He rubbed the brandy on her lips and gums, on the wrists, and the palms of her hands.

Meanwhile, I checked on the servants.

One of Lucy's dear friends, Quincey Morris, had also joined us from the adjoining house after he saw us enter through the kitchen window.

"We must have another blood transfusion, but the two of us are exhausted already," Van Helsing said to me.

Quincey gladly came forward to help.

Once again, Van Helsing carried out the operation. And once again, there seemed to be a slight improvement in Lucy's condition.

Later, we found Lucy's note in her pocket. On reading it, we were shocked and worried. Van Helsing kept the paper back in Lucy's pocket and said, "Forget it, for now. You will know and understand it all in good time."

I went out to make the funeral arrangements for Lucy's mother. When I returned, Lucy had woken up.

Her first instinct was to look in her pockets for the note that she had written, which Van Helsing had put back in its original place.

She looked around the room and smiled faintly when she saw us. She suddenly gave a loud cry when she realised that her dear mother was long dead. We consoled her as best as we could, and she wept silently and weakly for a long time.

In the evening, she slept uncomfortably.

But she also did a very odd thing. While still asleep, she took the note from her pocket and tore it into two. Van Helsing stepped over and took the pieces from her, but she went on with the action of tearing it as though the paper were still in her hands.

Van Helsing was surprised to see this and seemed to bein deep thought, but said nothing.

19 September

Van Helsing and I took turns to watch over Lucy and we never left her unattended. Arthur arrived early and was shocked to hear of the events. When he met Lucy, her spirits rose visibly.

I feel that tomorrow we will have to stop our watch. Lucy has had too great a shock. She cannot go on in this manner. God help us all.

Letter: Patrick Hennessey, MD to Dr Seward
20 September

My dear Sir,

Yesterday, an incident occurred regarding the patient Renfield. When he saw a cart heading towards the nearby deserted house, he grew restless and started shouting offensive words through the window.

Later, when he saw the cart leaving the house with some wooden boxes, he broke out of the window and attacked them.

He kept shouting, "I'll not let them rob me. I'll fight for my Lord and Master!" Thankfully, the people with the cart overpowered him before we reached there and we were able to take him back to his room.

Yours faithfully,

Patrick Hennessey

Dr Seward's Journal

20 September

Only habit forces me to write an entry tonight. Otherwise I am too miserable.

Lucy was clutching the garlic flowers tightly when she was awake, but had pushed them away in her sleep.

At 6 am, Van Helsing came to relieve me. He carefully examined Lucy, removed the flowers and looked at her throat. As he did so, he fell back and I could hear his exclamation, "My God!"

For a full five minutes, Van Helsing stood looking at her with an intense expression on his face. Finally, he turned to me and said, calmly, "She is dying. It will not be long now. Get Arthur, he must say his goodbyes."

When Arthur came in the room, Lucy opened her eyes and in a soft, tempting voice said, "Arthur! My love! I am so glad you have come! Kiss me!"

Arthur bent down eagerly to kiss her, but, in that instant, Van Helsing pulled him back with all his might and pushed him away from her.

"Not on your life!" he said. Arthur was so taken aback, he just looked on, nonplussed.

A look of rage passed like a shadow over Lucy's face. Then, she immediately calmed down and seemed more like herself. She looked at Van Helsing and said, "My true friend, and his!"

Lucy was quiet for some time and then said, "Guard him and give me peace, Professor."

Van Helsing knelt by her side, held her hand and said solemnly, "I swear, I will."

He gestured to Arthur, "Come, my child, take her hand in yours and kiss her on the forehead, and only once."

Arthur looked into Lucy's eyes and smiled softly. At that instant, Lucy's breathing grew heavy again and all at once, ceased.

"It's all over," Van Helsing said grimly. "She is dead."

I took Arthur downstairs where he broke down, sobbing as if he were ruined. When I got back to the room, Van Helsing was staring hard at Lucy, his eyes narrowed and brow furrowed.

Some changes had come over her body. She looked stronger somehow and her lips seemed to have regained colour.

"Ah well, it has ended at last," I said.

Van Helsing turned to me and, without a moment's thought, said, "Not so, alas! It is only the beginning!"

Chapter Ten

The Count Spotted in London

Dr Seward's Journal (continued)

The funeral was arranged for the next day so that both Lucy and her mother would be buried together. There weren't any relatives at hand and so we were unable to notify anyone in particular. Under these circumstances, Van Helsing and I took it upon ourselves to examine the papers, etc.

When the lawyer arrived, he informed us that Lucy's mother had already written her will as she had known that she was suffering from a weak heart. According to the will,

Arthur was supposed to inherit the estate and everything within.

The funeral went as planned and everybody who saw Lucy's body was surprised as to how beautiful and healthy she looked!

Later, Van Helsing pulled Arthur aside and said, "Do you know that all of Lucy's property is now yours?"

"No, I didn't. I have never even thought of it," Arthur replied.

"I want you to give me permission to read all of Miss Lucy's papers and letters. I think it will help me understand exactly what happened. It may shed some more light on the recent events."

"Dr Van Helsing, you may do what you will. I am sure Lucy would have approved of it."

Mina Harker's Journal

22 September

We were walking down the street at Piccadilly and Jonathan was holding my arm the way

he used to in the old days, when he suddenly squeezed my arm so tight that it ached.

I looked at him. Jonathan was alarmed and had stopped walking. He said under his breath, "My God!"

A sudden fear seemed to have gripped him. I followed his line of gaze and saw a tall, pale moustached man crossing the street.

"Do you know who that was?" he said in a terrified voice. "It is the Count himself. But he has grown younger, if that is possible."

For his sake, I took him home quickly and let him sleep off the trauma.

23 September

Jonathan is better after a bad night. I am glad he has plenty of work that keeps his mind off these terrible thoughts. I have decided to read Jonathan's account of his time in Transylvania.

I feel that the time has come to help him by sharing his burden.

Later

It's a sad homecoming in every way. Jonathan was still pale and dizzy following a relapse of his ailment and a telegram from a Dr Van Helsing arrived. It said, "You will be sad to hear that Lucy and her mother passed away day before yesterday. They were both buried today." Oh! what wealth of sorrow in so few words. Poor Lucy! Poor Arthur! God help us bear our troubles.

24 September

I didn't have the heart to write last night. Jonathan's record has left me upset and honestly, petrified. Poor dear! How he must have suffered.

Letter: Van Helsing to Mina Harker

Dear Madam,

I am sorry that I had to send you the sad news of Lucy's death. Due to Arthur's

kindness and help, I have gained access to her letters and journals, and am deeply concerned about a few important points.

By the love that you had for Lucy, I plead you to meet me so that we can talk about these things.

Van Helsing

Telegram: Mina Harker to Van Helsing

Come today. I can see you at any time.

Chapter Eleven

Lucy, the Vampire

Mina Harker's Journal

25 September

I cannot help feeling excited about Dr Van Helsing's visit, for somehow I expect that it will throw some light on Jonathan's sad, hair-raising experience. I have typewritten my own journal for him to read, which has all the details of my time with Lucy.

Later

He has come and gone. I feel like I am in a dream. Can it be possible? Poor Jonathan! How he must have suffered. I'll try and recollect exactly how the meeting went, for it might help to review a lot of facts.

When he came in, Van Helsing said, "It is on account of the dead that I come, Madam Mina"

"Sir," I said, for I wished to be of service to Lucy as I couldn't be of any in her life, "you will not find a better friend and helper of Lucy."

"I'll get straight to it then. I have read your letters to Miss Lucy and wish to know more about the days in which she was ill."

To which, I said, "I have typewritten a copy of my journal for you to read. It contains an accurate account of everything that happened during my time with Lucy."

I gave him the papers and at once he got down to reading them. Suddenly, he exclaimed, "Oh! Wonderful! This has thrown a lot of light into the facts of Lucy's case. Oh Madam! I am forever at your service. This is perfect."

He asked me how Jonathan was doing and I told him about the relapse yesterday. I pleaded with him to look into Jonathan's case, as it was troubling me a lot. He said, "You are lucky that his case is in my range of study. I will gladly look into his case too."

I immediately gave him a copy of Jonathan's journal from Transylvania. He seemed to be in a hurry and said, "I will take this along, Madam, and read it on the way back. I will telegram you what I think about it soon and will meet you tomorrow. Now, I will take your leave. I thank you again, for your help." With that he left.

Telegram: Van Helsing to Mina Harker

I have read your husband's journal. You may sleep without doubt. Strange and terrible as it is, it is true. He is a noble fellow and his experience was no disease!

Jonathan Harker's Journal

26 September

We met Van Helsing for breakfast. We spoke at length about a lot of things. He told me that

P-120

Lucy had been one of the Count's victims. We offered him all manner of help. Mina and I felt it was our moral duty to do so. Van Helsing said that he would send a telegram if he needed us.

Telegram: Van Helsing to Dr Seward, Arthur and Quincey

Friends, meet me at the graveyard tonight. We have some important work to do.

Dr Seward's Journal

29 September

Last night, we gathered near Lucy's tomb. Van Helsing said to us, "There is a grave duty to be done. I know you all thought that with Lucy's death, the horror has ended. But the fact is that we are yet to put an end to this, and I shall prove it to you."

We went inside Lucy's tomb, opened the coffin and looked in. To everyone's shock, it was empty!

"What does this mean?" Arthur asked.

Van Helsing gestured for us to wait outside, where he asked us to stay hidden. A little while later, we saw a white figure approaching the tomb. In the moonlight, it was clearly visible that the figure was none other than Lucy!

She looked stronger than we had ever seen her before and her teeth shone white in the moonlight. She seemed to glide through the door leading into the tomb!

We couldn't believe our eyes and were left speehless at this absurd spectacle.

Shedding some light on this mystery, Van Helsing said, "Lucy is now the undead. For the sake of her soul, we need to kill the vampire and let her soul find its place in heaven."

It was then that we all realised that Count Dracula was a vampire!

Now, Van Helsing looked directly at Arthur and said, "My dear friend Arthur, I think it is you who has to do this difficult task. Who

better than her one true love to save her from this cursed existence?"

Arthur was choked with emotion, but he finally said hoarsely, "Tell me what I am to do."

"Take this stake in your left hand, place it over the heart on Lucy's body and hammer it in with your right hand. We shall read from the Bible the Prayer for the Dead."

We entered the tomb just after dawn and Arthur did exactly as he was told. The rest of us read fervently from the Bible. The body in the coffin struggled for a while, when the stake hit the heart, and a hideous scream escaped from the open red lips. The body shook wildly and the mouth was soon frothy.

Arthur valiantly persevered through it all. Finally, with the last hammer blow, the body lay still and the terrible task was over.

Arthur fell down and we immediately helped him up.

For a few minutes, we took care of Arthur and we didn't look at the coffin. When we did, we were startled, as the face was that of the Lucy we had all known. It looked as if she was at peace, at last.

We left the tomb and got back to my house. When we were all settled, Van Helsing said, "Now, my friends, one step of our work is done. But there is still danger. We need to stamp out this evil from the face of the earth before it causes more harm. I am counting on you for your support."

We all nodded in agreement. We, too, felt that nobody should have to suffer the way we had at the hands of that cruel monster. No one should face the trouble that we had just faced.

30 September

Van Helsing informed me that Mr and Mrs Harker would be joining us in piecing together all the information that we have

about the Count. Mina had brought along her typewriter to write it all down, in order of the date. She thought that the dates were everything in this case and proceeded to place in order our individual notes into one main manuscript. Jonathan had, through his means, tracked down all the papers related to the Count's departure from Transylvania and his subsequent arrival in England.

The strangest thing that I learnt from all this was that the Count had bought the house next to my own! The fifty boxes had been delivered right next door.

Renfield was also somehow connected to the Count and his regular escapes to the deserted house now made some sense. The house belonged to the Count!

Chapter Twelve

Carafax

Mina Harker's Journal
29 September

Dr Van Helsing had been out, attending to other matters, and by the time he returned, I had finished making copies of all the facts in the case – arranged by date. I handed everyone a copy to read.

We all sat together at a large table, with Van Helsing at the head. He said, "I suppose now we are all familiar with the facts of the case?" We all nodded.

He went on, "Let me tell you more about the Count. He is a vampire who is not only stronger than ten men, but also has many magical powers. We have seen from these accounts that he can control wolves, bats, rats and many other animals. We have seen him transform himself into a wolf, a dog, a bat and also mist that can run through entire fields instantly. It may seem to us that this creature is the devil himself. But, there are certain rules that he has to follow.

"First, he can only work in the dark and he needs to be back in his coffin by sunrise. Second, he has to be invited into a place to go inside. Then, there are other things that he cannot handle, like the common garlic, the crucifix and also the sacred wafer. It seems we will have to use these symbols to send him back to Hell."

Van Helsing then paused and went on, "And now we must decide on our next course of action. We know from Jonathan's account that fifty boxes left Transylvania and Seward's colleague saw some of them being taken from the Count's house. We need to make sure if all the boxes have been carried out of the Count's house and I think we should do this tonight."

At that moment, the attendant came for Dr Seward and said that the patient, Renfield, had a special request to make. Knowing his connection to this case, we all went to his room.

Renfield surprised us with his good manners and logical thinking. He wanted to leave the asylum at once—he thought he was cured of his madness—as there was a matter that he wanted to urgently attend to. I didn't trust Renfield because I had seen how he could make logical claims and then throw a fit. Also, I somehow thought if he would be released, then he would try to help the Count in some way.

Van Helsing spoke up, "Mr Renfield, if you can tell us frankly the real reason that you have to leave right away, then we can think about letting you leave. Can you let us know?" At that, Renfield's face fell and he said, "No, I cannot. But let it be known that I tried to convince you. I hope you don't have any regrets later on."

We all left Renfield's room a little worried and got ready to make our trip next door to the Count's house. Everybody agreed that it would be safer if I stayed back in Seward's house.

Jonathan Harker's Journal
1 October

Van Helsing gave each of us a garland of garlic flowers and a piece of the sacred wafer for our mission. We all headed to the Count's place next door by climbing over the wall that separated the two estates.

Van Helsing had made a master key for the Count's main door. When we opened it, everybody took a step back out of fear.

Van Helsing crossed himself in prayer and said, "Into your hands, Lord!" and entered the Count's house.

It seemed to have been abandoned for centuries and everything was dusty. We looked for footprints showing us the direction in which

the boxes were taken and we reached a small chapel in the house.

Inside, we noticed that only twenty-nine of the original fifty boxes remained. Suddenly, we saw a lot of rats entering the chapel through a small hole in the wall. The number of rats just kept rising and we felt an evil presence in the chapel. We shuddered in fear. Arthur had thought of this situation. He took out a little silver whistle and blew a low shrill call. For a second, I thought I saw the Count's face through the open chapel door. But then it vanished.

I must be imagining things, I thought.

After about a minute, three dogs reached the chapel from the main door. They began to bite at the rats and chased them around, trying to disperse all the rats in the room.

It seemed to us that the evil presence just left the room when the dogs started barking. We all felt our spirits rise and suddenly, the atmosphere seemed to have been purified.

Van Helsing said, "So, we have found one other weapon against the Count. The rats were summoned by the Count, but he could do nothing against their instinct to run away from dogs. Or maybe the Count has gone somewhere."

After that, we returned to Dr Seward's house and I slept without waking up Mina.

Later

We all woke up later than usual due to all the fatigue following the visit to the Count's house. Mina, too, seemed exhausted, as I had to call her two or three times before she woke up. For a few seconds, her face had a look of blank terror, as if she had been woken up from a really bad dream. She complained that she was tired and I let her rest later in the day.

Mina Harker's Journal

1 October

Last night, I went to bed when the men had gone, simply because they told me to. I didn't

feel sleepy at all and I was thinking about all the things that had happened in the day.

I dreamt that I could hear dogs barking and a lot of other strange noises. It was one of those dreams that are a continuation of one's thoughts because I thought I saw a mist slowly move from the Count's house towards me. It came in under the door, and accumulated in the corner of the ceiling, like a fog. I thought I saw two red eyes look at me through the fog and I couldn't move my limbs. Things began to whirl in the room, and the last image I had was of a white face bending down, close to me out of the mist.

When I woke up, I saw that Jonathan had returned and that it was morning.

I should be more careful of the things I think of just before I go to bed. I think my fears are just acting up in my sleep.

For tonight, I have taken some medicine from Dr Seward that will help me sleep better, without dreams.

Chapter Thirteen

The Count Attacks Us

Jonathan Harker's Journal
2 October

I spent the last two days following up leads to locate the rest of the boxes. I found out that nine boxes were sent to a house in Piccadilly and the Count himself had taken the delivery. We have found another of his hideouts.

Dr Seward's Journal
1 October

I am puzzled about Renfield. His moods changed so rapidly that it has become difficult to understand his train of thoughts.

Today, I found him in a talkative mood. I kept talking to him about several subjects and he responded, but he did not mention his favourite topic—spiders, birds and flies. At one point, I asked him about the spiders and his reply shocked me. "I don't want any more spiders. I know I will get better things later."

Good Lord! I think the Count has been meeting him and promising him something.

Later

I placed a man in the corridor and told him to make an accurate note of any sound he might hear from Renfield's room.

After dinner, I was in my study when the attendant burst in and told me that Renfield had somehow met with an accident. He had heard him yell and when an attendant went inside, he found Renfield lying flat on his face on the floor, covered in blood.

I hurried to Renfield's room and found his body. I said to one of the attendants, "Go get Dr Van Helsing immediately!"

When Van Helsing came, he immediately took out his operating bag and sent the attendants away.

He said to me, "There is no time to lose. I can only give him a few minutes."

With that, Van Helsing proceeded to operate on his ear. Renfield's eyes suddenly opened and a few moments later, he smiled. Then said, "Doctor, I have something to say before I die."

He gasped for air and then went on, "He would come up to the window in a mist. He promised me rats, cats and dogs. All lives! All red blood! I found myself opening the window for him. Once, I saw Mrs Harker had come into the room too. She looked pale and I realised that he had been taking the life out of her.

"So tonight, I grabbed him tight, I did not want him to take blood from Mrs Harker. But he was stronger. He raised me up and flung me down. There was a noise, like thunder, and the mist seemed to go out from under the door."

His voice became softer and his breath more strained. Van Helsing stood up immediately, and said, "The Count is here and now we know his purpose. Perhaps it is not too late."

With that, we hurried to the Harkers' room. Arthur and Quincey also joined us. We found the door locked and we threw ourselves against it. With a crash the door burst open and we almost fell headlong into the room.

The scene there sickened us to the core.

Jonathan was lying on the ground breathing heavily, looking pale and exhausted. Mina Harker was kneeling next to the Count and was sucking blood out of his wrist! There was a look of devilish passion on the Count's face. He pushed Mina back onto the bed when he saw us and charged at us.

Immediately, Van Helsing held up the envelope that contained the sacred wafer right in front of him. The Count suddenly stopped and stepped back, a look of terror on his face.

He took another step back when we took out the crucifixes and walked towards him.

For a moment, the moon was covered by a dark cloud and we couldn't see anything. Quincey struck a match and we saw the mist escaping through the door. At that instant, Mina let out a scream of helplessness. Her face was white, with blood smeared all over her lips and cheeks.

Van Helsing said to me, "Jonathan is in a trance. Wake him up, immediately." Arthur and Quincey ran out behind the Count.

When Jonathan woke up, he was wild with anger. He said, "Doctor! Do something! Guard her while I look for him!"

Mina clung to Jonathan and cried, "No! No! Jonathan, you must not leave me."

After a while, Arthur and Quincey returned. Arthur was the first to speak, "The Count has burned all our papers. I looked in Renfield's room, but," he paused, "Renfield is dead!"

"God bless his poor soul!" said Van Helsing.

There was a pause before Quincey spoke, "I saw a bat rise from Renfield's window and flap westward, away from the next door house. He must be using some other hideout tonight."

Next, Van Helsing looked at Mina who seemed to have gained a bit of her old strength. He asked, "Mina, Can you tell us what happened?"

Mina sobbed as she spoke, "In the middle of the night, I woke up with a vague sense of fear, as if there was a presence in the room. I saw the Count emerging from the mist. I would have screamed, but I was paralysed. He pointed to Jonathan and spoke in a whisper, 'Silence! If you make a single sound, I will blow his brains out.' He paused and a smile crept up his face as he continued, 'First, I will refresh my thirst.'

"In my trance, I watched him place his lips on my neck and I felt my strength leave me. After a long while, he pulled back and spoke to me mockingly, 'And so you will fight me along

with the others, will you?' He looked even more angry at that point. 'Come now. I will put an end to this,' and with that he made a cut on his wrist, and his blood flowed out. He thrust his wrist onto my lips and made me drink from it. A short while later, you showed up."

Mina pulled Jonathan closer to her and sobbed uncontrollably.

After a while, Van Helsing spoke again, "You must rest now. One of us will stay with you for the night and guard you. There is nothing more that can be done tonight."

Chapter Fourteen

Purifying The Houses

Dr Seward's Journal

3 October

In the morning, after breakfast, we all gathered at the table again.

Van Helsing said, "It is a good thing that when we were next to the Count's house, we did not purify his boxes. He doesn't know our plan and so we can carry it out today.

"Once we have purified the boxes next door, we must move to his house in Piccadilly and find out about the other places where he must have purchased properties. Then, we can purify all the other boxes as well."

"Come on, let us leave at once," I cried. "We shouldn't waste any more precious time! Who knows how many other lives are at stake?"

We left Mina at home, with every precaution taken to foil any attempt by the Count to gain entry. When we reached the Count's house, we found the boxes just as we had left them—all twenty-nine of them. Immediately, we began purifying the boxes by putting the sacred wafer inside the dirt in the boxes. This was hard work because all the boxes were nailed shut.

When we were done, we immediately moved to the Count's house in Piccadilly. Our plan was to break into the house using a locksmith. Arthur and Quincey were going to act as if they were the owners of the house and had lost their keys. Then, they had to calmly pay off the locksmith, so that we would gain entry into the place.

When this was done, we entered the place, and found only eight boxes there. We immediately purified the boxes with the sacred wafer and looked for any clues that could tell us where his other houses were.

Until now we hadn't seen the Count and assumed that he was in one of his other houses.

After searching for a while, we found a set of documents and a bunch of keys in the house. At that moment, there was a knock on the door and we got a telegram from Mina.

Telegram: Mina to Jonathan, Piccadilly

I have just seen the Count leave his house that's next door to ours and hurry south towards the Piccadilly house. Take care.

Mina

Everyone was lost in thought, when Arthur said, "Let's do this. Quincey and I will go to the other two houses to purify them and the three of you wait here for the Count." We all nodded in agreement.

After about an hour, there was a knock on the door. We jumped to attention. Van Helsing slowly made for the door and held up his crucifix. When we opened the door, we found that it was Arthur and Quincey!

They quickly came in and closed the door. Quincey said, "It is all right. We found both places easily. Six boxes in each of them and we purified them all. That leaves us with just one box, which we couldn't find."

Van Helsing spoke, "We will wait for him here till five and then we must leave. It would not be good to leave Mina alone after sunset."

At that moment, we heard the key being turned in the door. We waited in chilling suspense. The seconds seemed to pass with nightmarish sluggishness. The Count was moving slowly because evidently he was prepared for some surprise.

Suddenly, in a single leap, he jumped into the room. He ran past us, his movement

almost animal-like. Harker was the first to act. He threw himself at the door blocking the Count's exit.

As the Count saw us, there was anger and an evil look on his face which quickly turned into a cold, wild stare. With a single movement, all of us advanced upon him. It was a pity that we did not have a more organised plan of attack because, in that moment, we were all wondering what we could do next.

Again, Harker moved first and took out a knife and tried to slash the Count with a fierce movement. It was a powerful attack, but the quickness with which the Count leapt back, saved him from any injury. The expression on the Count's face was hellish, mixed with what appeared to be fear.

Impulsively, Van Helsing moved closer to the Count with the crucifix and sacred wafer in his hand. The Count took another step back and the pale face turned a horrible greenish-yellow.

Harker took another swipe at the Count and this time, he managed to cut the Count's jacket, and out fell a bundle of currency notes and a stream of gold. In the next instant, the Count jumped under Harker's outstretched arm, picked a handful of the money from the floor and threw himself at the window. With a loud crash of glass and the tinkle of some fallen gold, the Count fell into the yard below.

He turned and screamed at us, his face twisted into lines of deep hatred, "You think you have found all my resting places, but I have more. My revenge has just begun. The girls that you love are mine already, and through them, you will all be mine. You will all be my slaves and will do as I say! I am immortal!"

He had fallen down to the stables. He quickly passed through a door and we heard a rusty bolt creak, as he fastened it behind him.

Van Helsing spoke first, "We have learnt something. Despite his brave words, he fears

us. If not, then why did he hurry out? His tone betrayed him. And why take the money? You must try and follow him from the front door while I clear out anything from here that may be of use to him."

Arthur and Quincey rushed out to the garden. Harker lowered himself from the window to the stable and I ran outside to the back door, trying to see if someone had seen him outside. But the footpaths were deserted and no one had seen him leave.

It was now late in the afternoon and it would soon be sunset. We recognised that our time was up and we had to get back to Mina.

Van Helsing said urgently, "Let us go back immediately. All we could do, is done and we must protect Mina. Now there is only one more box left, and we must try and find it. When that is done, all may be well."

With heavy hearts we returned to my house, where we found Mina waiting for us with a cheerfulness that brought smiles on our faces.

For a second or two, her eyes were closed, as if she were saying a prayer and then she said with a smile, "I can never thank you all enough. Oh, my poor darling!" As she spoke, she took Jonathan's head in her hands and kissed it. "Lay your poor head here and rest. God will protect us, if he thinks it is right. And if we are to win against this evil, well, God will help us do that too." The poor fellow groaned in sadness.

We had dinner together and got ready for bed. Van Helsing fixed up the room to protect against any vampire attack and assured Mina that she would sleep in peace. Again, we took turns to watch over the Harkers, just to be sure.

Jonathan Harker's Journal

4 October, morning

I was woken up by Mina just before dawn. She seemed to be caught in a storm. She said to me hurriedly, "Go, call Van Helsing. I have an idea and I want to see him at once."

I went to the door. Dr Seward was resting on the mattress and on seeing me, he sprang to his feet.

"Is anything wrong?" he asked, in alarm.

"No," I replied. "But Mina wants to see Van Helsing at once."

In two or three minutes, Van Helsing was in the room in his dressing gown with Arthur, Quincey and Dr Seward.

When Van Helsing saw Mina, the smile on her face put to rest all our worries. She said, "I want you to hypnotise me."

"Do it before the dawn, for I feel that then I can speak freely. Be quick, for time is short. Please hurry!" Without a word, he motioned her to sit up in bed.

Looking intensely at her, he took out his pocket watch and moved it to and fro, like a pendulum, in front of her eyes. Mina stared back at him. Gradually, her eyes closed and she sat absolutely still. Van Helsing stopped

moving his pocket watch. Mina opened her eyes, but they seemed different somehow, they had a far away look. In fact, Mina herself somehow seemed different.

Van Helsing spoke in a low voice, so as to not disturb her, "Where are you?"

The answer came dreamily, but with intention. It was like she was trying to understand where she was. "I can see nothing. It is all dark."

"What do you hear?" Van Helsing asked.

"I can hear the waves leap. I can hear water all around me."

"Then, you are on a ship?" he asked hopefully.

"Yes!" she said.

"What are you doing?"

"I am still, very still."

Her voice faded away; she sighed deeply, and then shut her eyes again.

After a moment, she woke up, as if from a deep sleep, and looked around.

Van Helsing spoke, after a few moments of thought over what Mina had said, "Ah! So the Count is at sea! That is why he took the money. He meant to escape. He has seen that with only one box left and us on his heels, there was only one plausible option—retreat. I think, he knows he has no chance of winning this time. We should follow him at once!"

Quincey said, "But why should we follow him? He won't hurt us anymore."

Van Helsing replied, "Because he can live for centuries. He can outlive us all. And now, since he has bitten Mina, we have to kill him or he will get her soul when she dies."

Chapter Fifteen

Mina's Promise

Dr Seward's Journal

4 October

Today, Arthur returned with news about the ship that the Count has taken.

The ship's name is the *Czarina* and is bound for Verna. Van Helsing calculated the time of arrival at port to be a minimum of two weeks, since it will be taking the river route through the Danube. He calculated our own travel, if undertaken by ship and then by road, to be less than four days. We are to prepare for our travel immediately.

Quincey bribed the shipping company to keep him informed everyday about the whereabouts of the ship.

We seemed to be in a country where bribes could get us everywhere.

Mina is changing fast. She looks stronger, more robust and her teeth are unnaturally whiter. She is silent and tired all day. She looked like she was being held back by something.

I fear that the Count's hold on her is tightening.

We all agreed that for her sake, the Harkers be left behind for this most dangerous quest of ours. Mina seemed to understand our decision and wished us well.

Today in the evening, she called us all to her room. Nowadays, she seems to be able to talk freely only during sunrise or sunset because that is the time the Count's power over her weakens.

Mina spoke slowly, but surely, "I know that you all are going into danger and you want me to be safe."

She paused for a moment, looked directly at Van Helsing, and said, "I think I should come along with you on this journey."

Van Helsing said, "But Mina, you know that this is a perilous expedition. Unfortunately, the devil has you under his control. I think you staying overseas is a good thing, he will not be able to have much effect on you."

Mina nodded and said confidently, "I know that when the Count calls me, I must go. But I think that, in itself, is a very good reason for me to travel with you. I can be of help; you can hypnotise me to get information about the whereabouts of the Count."

Van Helsing smiled, understanding the logic and said gravely, "Madam Mina, you are, as always, very wise! You shall come with us."

Though we could see she was getting tired now, Mina continued, "But mind you, if I can look into his mind and understand what he is up to, then he too has the power to see what

I am up to. It would be better, if you do not share any of your plans with me. Jonathan, you shouldn't tell me about anything related to this trip either."

Jonathan looked at her sadly and said, "I promise that I won't, Mina."

Mina sobbed a bit, suddenly stopped and tried to compose herself before she said, "And there is another thing that I want all of you to promise me. If you think that I am beyond hope and that I have already crossed over to the other side, then...then I want you to kill me and cut my head off."

There was stunned silence at this very strange request.

She paused for a moment and continued, "I know that it is too much to ask of people who care for me, but I want to know that my life will be in the hands of the people I love, and not at the mercy of the Count."

Sobbing, she continued, "You have told me of what happened with Lucy. I would like that

if I do go over to the Count's side, then my beloved Jonathan will be the one to send me to my heavenly abode and if he is unavailable, then one of you, my friends, will give me peace."

With that, she looked around. All of us had tears in our eyes.

Quincey spoke, "I promise, Madam Mina, that I will do as you wish, but I also promise to do all that I can, all that is within my power, to ensure that the Count will be finished before he can hurt you."

We all nodded in agreement. We took each other's hands and prayed in silence for a minute.

Tomorrow, we set sail.

Chapter Sixteen

The Pursuit

Jonathan Harker's Journal
15 October, Varna

Until the *Czarina* comes to port, we will need to wait for her here. It has become a habit of Van Helsing to hypnotise Mina before sunrise. He always asks her two questions: what she can see and what she can hear.

To the first, she answers, "Nothing. All is dark." And to the second, "I can hear the waves touching the ship, the creaking and straining of the mast, and the sails of the ship."

It is clear that the *Czarina* is still on her way to Varna.

24 October

We have been waiting a whole week for the ship. It is clear to us that the Count has some surprise for us. Today, we got a telegram that the *Czarina* has been reported from Dardanelles.

She is late, but seems to be heading right at us. We have arranged to board the ship as soon as she reaches the port. You can get everything done here for the right amount of bribe.

Dr Seward's Journal

25 October, Noon

It is only a 24-hour sail from Dardanelles to here, at the rate that she is travelling. We wait for her at port. Jonathan is always sharpening and practising with his knife. A fierce power seems to fuel him. Perhaps, it is in preparation for revenge at the treatment meted to him by the Count. Or maybe Mina's recent disposition is the reason. I fear for the man who goes up against Jonathan.

The rest are feverishly excited.

I think this is how a man must feel when he is about to go to war. Madam Mina seems brighter and better than she has been for days. She still reports the same scene when hypnotised. Somehow her cheery attitude scares me. I fear it is something related to the Count.

28 October

We received a telegram today that the *Czarina* had entered Galatz. It was a bit of a shock to us that the ship didn't come to Varna and went ahead. But we had expected something different from the Count. Everyone seems frustrated with the new turn of events.

Van Helsing asked, "When does the next train start for Galatz?"

"At 6:30, tomorrow morning," Mina replied, promptly.

Arthur and Quincey left to make the travel arrangements and to secure as much help as we could get in Galatz.

Van Helsing asked Mina, "Tell me, Mina, how do you feel?"

Mina spoke at once, "I think that the Count found out that we were here, looking at what I could see and hear in the same way as I was doing for you. He realised that having me as his servant is not helping him and so he has cut me off from him. Oh! Thank God for His mercy! My soul is freer than it has been since that awful day. I think that is the reason why I am feeling so much better lately."

Van Helsing stood up and said, "He has used your mind, left us at Varna and rushed to Galatz. He also thinks that because he has cut himself off from reading your mind, you will be unable to read his. But because his blood is in your blood stream, you can still go into his mind as you take my orders and not his. We will keep up the practice of hypnotising you at sunrise and sunset, till we face him."

29 October

We are on a train from Varna to Galatz. Van Helsing again tried to hypnotise Mina, but this time it took a lot more effort on his part. At last, she said, "I can see nothing. We are still and I can hear a steady flow of water around me. I can hear men's voices calling. There is sound of heavy foot steps overhead, and ropes and chains are being dragged along. What is this? There is a glow of light. I can feel the air blowing upon me."

Here, she stopped and woke up as if from a deep sleep.

Van Helsing said, "I think he is close to land. He has left his box, but he is yet to go on shore. He will need to be carried onshore, but he has to do this when the customs personnel are not watching. We may still arrive on time."

At sunset, Van Helsing tried again. It was getting more difficult to hypnotise her, but at

last, she said, "I can hear confused sounds of men talking in strange languages, fierce falling water and the howling of wolves." For a few seconds, she shook violently, like she was in a fit, and woke up with a start immediately. She asked what she had said and sat thinking about it for a long time.

30 October

We are near Galatz now, and I may not be able to write later. Everyone is waiting for the sunrise, as we could know more of the Count's location.

Again, Van Helsing took a long time to hypnotise her and eventually she said, "All is dark. I can hear flowing water and creaking of wood on wood. I can hear the distant sound of cattle." With that, she woke up with a start.

The whistles are sounding. We are nearing Galatz.

Jonathan Harker's journal

30 October

We met with the Captain of the *Czarina*. He gave us an interesting account of how the ship was having great luck with the winds helping them. He said, "Me didn't want to anger the Gods and hence, me let the wind take the ship to wherever it wanted to take us to. When the wind stopped, me found us on the shore to Galatz. It was early in the morning, and a gypsy man came with the papers to collect the box marked for a Count Dracula. Me knew that the gypsy men wanted to save on port fees and so, me give them the box."

We thanked the Captain with money for the information and got back to the hotel.

Mina was deep in thought when we returned. She was reading all our diary entries and also checking up on the maps of the area. Suddenly, she smiled and asked me to get the rest of them.

When everyone was present, she started, "I have examined the map and found that the river most suitable to reach the Count's castle is the Sereth. I read in the typescript that during my trance I heard cows moo, water flowing and the creaking of wood. The Count, in his box, was on a river in an open boat, probably a boat with oars. With that, he will have avoided the roads, as that will lead to many questions and will reach as close to his castle as possible.

When she was finished, I quickly took her in my arms and gave her a kiss. The others patted her back and Van Helsing said, "Our dear Madam Mina, is once again our teacher. She sees what we do not."

He thought for a while and added, "The Count will not make himself visible to the gypsy people. If he does, then they will promptly throw him in the stream to his death. That is why he is now at the mercy of their speed. Now, we must decide what our next course of action should be."

Arthur said, "I will get a steamboat and follow him."

Quincey added, "And I will follow on the bank of the river if, by chance, the Count decides to land."

Van Helsing said, "Good, but no one must go alone. The gypsy people are strong and they may be armed."

Seward said, "I will join Quincey then."

Van Helsing then looked at me and said, "Jonathan, then you must go with Arthur. I don't think that I am young enough for a pursuit. I will take Mina and head to the Castle Dracula in a carriage. It will help to know of the Count's movements by hypnotising Mina."

I interrupted him angrily, "Do you mean to say that you will bring Mina, in her state with the devil's illness, right into his death trap? Not for the world."

I felt a surge of fear mixed with emotion and sat down on the sofa.

Van Helsing spoke in a clear, sweet voice, which seemed to calm all of us, he said, "Oh my friend, it is because I would save Mina from that awful place. There is wild work to be done before that place can be purified. If the Count escapes us, he could sleep for a century and then, in time, Mina will join the other ladies in the castle waiting for the Count to give them babies to eat in a sack."

He paused, for the horrible picture to set in my mind, and continued, "I am sorry I have to say it this way, but it is necessary. We are all playing with our lives here, Jonathan."

I choked up, overwhelmed at this point, and said, "Do as you will. God be with us!"

Later

I am glad we have such rich, loving and brave people with us. Arthur and Quincey have already spent a fortune. If it wasn't for them,

we could not have started so quickly and been so well equipped in an hour.

Arthur and I leave on the steam boat with Quincey and Seward galloping with a good half a dozen horses.

Mina and Van Helsing will first take a train to Bistritz from where they will hire a carriage. We are all well armed for the fight, as we begin the final leg of our journey. It could well be our last few days.

Chapter Seventeen

The Castle Conquered

Jonathan Harker's Journal
30 October, night

I am writing this on the steamboat that Arthur hired. He is an experienced boatman and we speed up the river with no hindrances.

We are hurrying along and we found a few boats on the river, but none of them had the heavy box on them.

The cold is creeping up as we ride along and I am feeling very sleepy.

I wonder where Mina and Van Helsing are right now. I hope they are doing well. I pray fervently for my love. Let nothing harm her.

Mina Harker's Journal

31 October

Today, we arrived at Bistritz at noon. Van Helsing told me that this morning, he could hardly hypnotise me and that all I could say was, "dark and quiet".

We still have a long way to go and the countryside is so beautiful that I would have loved to come here in different circumstances.

Van Helsing procured all that we needed for the ride and we left immediately.

I am afraid to think what will happen to us, but I must remain strong.We are travelling fast and it is getting colder as we near the Count's castle.

2 November, morning

We took turns riding the carriage and we both are in good spirits. At dawn, Van Helsing hypnotised me and asked me what I saw. I replied, "Darkness, creaking wood and roaring water." This means, the river is growing stronger. I do hope that my darling Jonathan has not yet met with any danger.

Abraham Van Helsing's Journal
4 November

This is to my old friend John Seward, in case I don't see him. I am writing this because Mina seems to have stopped writing her journal. She just sleeps and sleeps. It is getting colder as we go on. I suppose that must have affected her. She has also lost her appetite, which I do not like. I will have to keep an eye on her. I will let her sleep, but I cannot sleep in the night.

Some new guiding power seems to have grown in her because she pointed to a road and said, "This is the way."

I asked her, "How do you know?"

She said, "Of course I know it," she paused and added, "It was in Jonathan's journal, was it not?"

I let go of the reins and the horses go on patiently. Mina sleeps and sleeps. I tried to wake her once, but she didn't wake up. A little while later, I thought it would be a good time to stop for some food. Then again, I tried to wake Mina and she woke up immediately.

She looked very healthy and bright.

I tried to hypnotise her, but failed. The sun had set so I couldn't do more, but she got up and laughed brightly. I offered her food, but she didn't want it.

I then tried to sleep for a while, but I felt like someone was watching me. When I opened my eyes, I saw Mina staring right at me. I don't want to point it out to her and scare her, but I think she is turning more and more into a vampire, as we approach the Count's castle.

November 5

We travelled all day and we reached near the top of the hill, where I think the castle stands.

I made a fire and made Mina sit all cosy with rugs. I tried to hypnotise her, but couldn't. I offered her food, but she doesn't seem to want it. I eat because I need the strength. Then, I broke the sacred wafer and made a large ring around her. I said, "Will you not come over to the fire?"

She tried to take a step, but couldn't; she stood like a statue. Again, I asked her, "Why not go on?" She looked at me and said simply, "I cannot."

Later

For the first time, I have felt closer to the Count's evil powers since starting this journey. The horses started screaming and tore at their ropes until I went to them and soothed them. Then in the snow, I thought, I saw a mist with the three women that Jonathan wrote of in his journal. I immediately went inside the ring that I made for Mina. After a few minutes, the fire seemed to die and I stepped out to replenish it,

when Mina caught me and whispered, "No! No! Do not go outside. Here you are safe."

Then, the women began to materialise till I saw them just as Jonathan had described in his journal. They said in sweet, tingling tones, "Come, sister. Come to us. Come."

In fear, I turned to look at Mina and my heart smiled instantly. She seemed just as scared of them. *Thank God! She is not yet one of them.*

They laughed their cruel laugh, and retreated. I noticed that the horses had stopped moaning and lay still on the ground. The snow fell on them softly and they grew whiter.

We stayed like that till dawn. I was full of terror, but when the beautiful sun began to climb the horizon, I was filled with life.

Mina was sleeping and I tried to hypnotise her in her sleep, but failed. Then I saw that the horses were all dead.

The sunlight is my safety as I make way to the castle. Mina sleeps and God be thanked. She is calm in her sleep.

Jonathan Harker's Journal
4 November, evening

Our steam launcher met with an accident. If that hadn't happened, then we might have overtaken the boat long ago and Mina would have been free by now.

We have got horses and we follow on the set track. We have our rifles, should the gypsy people attack us. We must keep hope. If I write no more, consider this my goodbye, Mina. God bless and keep you.

Dr Seward's Journal
5 November

At dawn, we saw the gypsy people hurrying away with a large cart. They had surrounded it as if they were protecting the cart. The snow is falling lightly and there is a strange excitement in the air as we wait for our horses to be ready.

After a while, we begin our pursuit. We ride to death. God alone knows whose death.

Van Helsing's Journal

5 November, afternoon

I left Mina sleeping and made my way to the castle. The blacksmith's hammer serves me well. When I reach the castle, I find the doors open, but I still break the rusty hinges, lest I find them closed when I return. I head straight for the Old Chapel because that is where Jonathan said the tombs were. I can hear the sound of wolves outside and I worry for Mina. But then, I let God take care of her.

I knew there were at least three filled graves to be found and I went searching for them. When I found the first grave, I discovered that there was a beautiful woman inside it. She looked very pretty and I couln't help but wonder, how any man would find it in his heart to kill such a beautiful woman. I wondered if there had been another man who might have tried to kill these vampires, but on seeing them, his heart faltered and he was hypnotised till sunset. Then, they

would have woken up and given him the kiss of death.

Suddenly, my thoughts were interrupted by a long, shrill cry which, I was sure, was from Madam Mina! I went on ahead and found the other two tombs, and finally found another high tomb, marked in large letters, 'DRACULA'.

Then, began the terrible task of killing the three women and any hesitation was broken by the thought of the cry from Madam Mina.

Oh! It was butcher work. Thank God! My nerves withstood it. As I finished with each one, it was as if Time itself caught up with them and they perished in a puff of dust. It was like Death itself said, "I am here!"

I immediately started purifying the whole castle. I began with the Count's grave in which I placed a sacred wafer. Before I left the castle, I barricaded all the entrances, so that the Count could never enter it. When I stepped into the circle where Madam Mina was sleeping, she

woke up. Upon seeing me, she said, "Come, let us go and meet my husband who is, I know, coming to me."

She looked pale and thin, but her eyes were pure and glowed. And so with trust and hope, we go eastward to meet our friends.

Mina Harker's Journal

6 November

It was late afternoon when Van Helsing and I moved downwards, down the steep hill. We did not go fast, since it was cold and snowing. I was tired with the heavy walking and sat down to rest. Van Helsing found a wonderful spot between two boulders. He said, "See! Here you will be sheltered. If the wolves come, then I can meet them one by one."

Taking his field glasses from the case, he stood on top of the rock and began to search the horizon.

Chapter Eighteen

Dracula is Dead

Mina Harker's Journal (continued)

Van Helsing kept looking at the horizon using his field glasses.

Suddenly, he called out, "Look! Madam Mina, Look!"

I sprang up and stood beside him. He handed me the glasses and pointed. The snow was still falling and I could only see in pauses, when the snowfall stopped. And far off, beyond the white waste of snow, I could see the river. Straight in front of us and not far off was a group of mounted men hurrying along. In their midst, was a cart on which was a great square chest.

My heart leapt, as I felt that the end was coming. The evening was ending soon too. I knew that if we didn't end it soon, then the Count would become all powerful.

I looked to my side and saw that Van Helsing was now making the ring around us with the fine, sacred wafer.

He immediately joined me again on the rock and excitedly pointed south, and said, "See! See! Two horsemen were clearly riding fast towards the gypsies. It must be Quincey and Dr Seward. Take the glass. Look! before the snow blocks your view."

I looked again and my first thought was that neither of them was Jonathan. But, I also knew that Jonathan was not far away. Looking towards the north of the gypsy men, I saw two men riding hard. One of them was Jonathan, and the other was clearly Arthur. When I showed this to Van Helsing, he shouted out in glee and took out his rifle ready for use.

"They are all converging," he said. I was armed like the rest of them, so I took out my revolver and readied it because the howling of the wolves was inching closer.

It was strange to see the snow falling heavily near us, and beyond the sun shining more and more brightly as it sank down into the far mountain tops. Sweeping the glass around us, I could see here and there dots moving in twos and threes, and in larger numbers. The wolves were gathering for their prey.

Time, it seems, had stood still as we waited for the final confrontation. But it seemed that no one had noticed our presence.

All at once, two voices shouted out, "Halt!" One was that of my Jonathan and the other was that of Quincey. The leader of the gypsies barked out commands to his men and they whipped their horses to gain speed. The four men raised their rifles and, without mistake, commanded them to stop. At the same instant,

Van Helsing and I rose behind the rock and pointed our weapons to them.

Seeing that they were surrounded, the gypsies stopped and drew out whatever weapons they had. The leader first pointed to the sun setting in the mountains and then pointed towards the castle, and said something which I did not understand. All the men threw themselves off their horses and dashed towards the cart.

Surprisingly, I felt no fear, only a wild desire to do something. Perhaps, it was the adrenaline. Perhaps, it was a combination of all the atrocities we had suffered at the hands of this vicious vampire. But at that point, I felt no fear. I could see this reflected in the eyes of the brave men around me.

The leader again barked an order, and the others formed a ring around the cart with their backs to it. I saw Jonathan on one side of the ring of men and Quincey on the other.

Jonathan charged rashly, with single-minded purpose, and the men, fearing his wrath, let him pass. In an instant, he was on the cart and with a strength, which seemed incredible, raised the great box and flung it over the wheel to the ground. Meanwhile, Quincey resorted to force to get through his side of the ring of men. Though he slashed and pierced fiercely, the gypsies fought back.

He continued to swing and charge at the gypsies with his knife and, in a flash, made his way through them. As he sprang to the side of Jonathan, who had now jumped from the cart, I noticed that he was clutching his left side and blood was oozing through his fingers. My heart was wild with fear for my husband, but I somehow managed to hold myself steady.

Then, both of them attempted to open the lid of the great box with their knives. They worked with the ferocity of the possessed. It didn't take long. The nails drew out with a

screeching sound and the lid of the box was thrown back.

By this time, the gypsies, surrounded by the rifles, had given up. The sun was almost down from the mountain top and I saw the Count lying inside the box on the ground. He seemed very pale and his red eyes glared with a cruel look that we were all familiar with by now.

His eyes saw the sinking sun and the look of hate immediately turned into one of triumph. He knew that upon sunset, all our combined efforts would amount to nothing before his evil powers.

But at that instant, came the sweep and flash of Jonathan's great knife that sunk deep into his throat. I shrieked, as I saw it pierce through the throat. In the same instant, Quincey quickly plunged his knife into the Count's heart with all his might.

It was like a miracle, but before our very eyes, and almost at the drawing of a breath, his whole body crumbled to dust and vanished from our sight. It just seemed to become one with the air.

I shall be glad, as long as I live, that even in that moment of final dissolution, there was in that face a look of peace, such as I expected.

The Castle Dracula now stood out against the red sky, and every stone of its broken battlements thrown into sharp relief against the light of the setting sun.

The gypsies, scared of the extraordinary disappearance of the dead man, turned and rode away without a word, as if they feared we would turn on them next. Those who had unmounted earlier, shouted out to the horsemen not to leave them behind.

The wolves that had withdrawn to a safe distance, followed in their wake and left us alone.

Quincey lay on the ground, leaning on his elbow. I cried out, for I couldn't help it.

I knew Quincey, our brave comrade, had been gravely injured. He had only moments to live. We all ran towards him. Jonathan knelt behind him and Quincey laid his head on his shoulder. He took my hand and said, "I am only too happy to have been of service."

Suddenly, he pointed to me and cried, "It was all worth it. Look! Look!"

The setting sun sent red flames upon my face so that I was bathed in rosy light. And they saw that I had gone back to my previous, healthy self. I was free of the devilry which had ruled me, so far.

Quincey said with his last breath, "Thank God all our effort has not been in vain! The curse has passed!"

And, to our sorrow, with a smile on his face, he died, a gallant gentleman.

Chapter Nineteen

Note

Seven years ago, we all went through the fires of Hell. But, the happiness of some of us since then, in our opinion, is almost worth the pain we endured. It is an added joy to Mina and to me that our boy's birthday is the same day as that on which Quincey Morris, our dear, brave friend, died. We have named him Quincey, after the bravest of our friends.

His mother ardently believes that the little boy has a great deal of his namesake's spirit. He too is a courageous and energetic fellow.

In the summer of this year, we made a journey to Transylvania, and went over the old ground which was, and is, to us so full of vivid and terrible memories.

It was almost impossible to believe that the things we had seen with our own eyes and heard with our own ears were living truths. Every trace of all that had been was blotted out. But Castle Dracula stood as before, towering above a waste of desolation.

Arthur and Seward are both happily married, and all that remains of our trials is a mass of material, typewritten and some handwritten. We realised there is no official document in there. Only our memoirs, most of them hastily jotted down in a bid to be remembered, if the writer were unceremoniously dead.

Without official proof, nobody would really believe this almost fantastic tale of ours. But, we know we have rid humanity of one of the darkest evils ever seen.

Van Helsing summed it all up as he said, with our boy on his knee, "We have no proof. We ask no one to believe us. This boy will someday know what a brave and gallant woman his mother is. And how so many dared so much for her sake."

Jonathan Harker

About the Author

■ Abraham "Bram" Stoker

Abraham "Bram" Stoker was born on 8 November 1847 at Clontarf, Dublin in Ireland. His parents attended the Parish Church of Clontarf with their children. Stoker was the third of seven children.

Stoker was bedridden of an unknown illness till the age of seven when he made a complete recovery. Stoker wrote, "I was naturally thoughtful and the leisure of long illness gave opportunity for many thoughts which gave fruit in my later years."

Later, he became a university athlete at Trinity College, Dublin.

Stoker became interested in theatre through a friend, Dr Maunsell. He later became a critic for the *Dublin Evening Mail*. He gained popularity because of the quality of his reviews.

He is most famous for his book, *Count Dracula*. But during his lifetime, he was better known as the personal assistant of actor Henry Irving and as the business manager of the Lyceum Theatre.

Count Dracula is an epistolary novel, written as a collection of realistic, but completely fictional, diary entries, telegrams, letters, ship's logs, and newspaper clippings, all of which added a level of detailed realism to his story, a skill he developed as a newspaper writer.

An annual festival takes place in Dublin, the birthplace of Bram Stoker, in honour of his literary achievements.

Stoker died due to multiple strokes at the age of 64.

▪ Characters

Count Dracula: He is the villain after who the novel is named. He is a vampire, a creature who drinks blood to survive. He is a nobleman who has survived for centuries because he is a vampire. He is physically very strong and can use magic to control and change into a lot of animals. He wants to move to a large city like London to feast on the blood of many people and is successful for a while. He is eventually defeated by some really clever people.

Jonathan Harker: A lawyer working in England, he is sent by his company to help purchase a house for the Count. He escapes from the Count's castle. Later, he is one of those who vanquish the Count.

Mina Harker: She is the wife of Jonathan Harker. She is the childhood friend of Lucy Westenra. She is a very clever woman and the main female protagonist of the story.

Professor Dr Abraham Van Helsing: He is an old professor and current friend of John Seward. He researches never-seen-before diseases. He is the mastermind of the whole story and a father-figure to all.

Lucy Westenra: The beautiful lady engaged to be married to Arthur Holmwood, she becomes the first victim of the Count in England.

Arthur Holmwood: The rich fiancé of Lucy. His father is a Lord and hence he has a lot of connections. He is a friend of Quincey Morris and John Seward. He is one of the financers of the whole mission to vanquish Dracula.

Dr John Seward: He is a doctor by profession. He owns an estate which he has converted into a mental asylum. He is a friend of Arthur. He studied under Professor Van Helsing.

Quincey Morris: He is an American. He is a friend of Arthur, Seward and Lucy. He is eventually killed in action.

Renfield: He is a madman admitted in Dr Seward's asylum. He likes animals and sometimes eats them. He wants to be Count Dracula's slave.

Dracula's three beautiful ladies: They are Count Dracula's companions. They have an alluring voice, but Van Helsing eventually kills them.

■ Questions

Chapter 1

- *When does the old woman let Jonathan go?*
- *Describe Jonathan's trip from the inn to Count Dracula's castle?*

Chapter 2

- *Why does the Count grab Jonathan's throat?*
- *Why are there no exits in the castle?*

Chapter 3

- *How many boxes are there?*
- *What is in the sack?*

Chapter 4

- *What do Mina and Lucy see at the docks?*
- *How is Arthur related to Lucy?*

Chapter 5

- *What is Renfield's hobby?*
- *What happens on the night that Renfield escapes?*

Chapter 6

- *What does Lucy dream about?*
- *What does Mina do with Jonathan's journal?*

Chapter 7

- *Why does Lucy need a blood transfusion?*
- *What kind of flowers does Van Helsing give Lucy?Why?*

Chapter 8

- *What does Lucy's mother do that annoys Van Helsing?*
- *What crashes through the window?*

Chapter 9

- *What do Van Helsing and Seward first see on arriving at Lucy's house?*
- *What kind of efforts are made to save Lucy?*

Chapter 10

- *How does Lucy look at her funeral?*
- *What does Jonathan see on the streets that terrifies him?*

Chapter 11

- *What does Van Helsing say to Mina after reading the journal?*
- *What happens at Lucy's tomb?*

Chapter 12

- *What does Seward say at the Chapel door?*
- *What does Arthur do to take care of the rats?*

Chapter 13

- *Why does Renfield fight the count?*
- *What does the Count make Mina do?*

Chapter 14

- *What does the Count grab before he runs?*
- *How many houses did the Count have in England?*

Chapter 15

- *Describe Mina's condition.*
- *What does Mina make everyone promise?*

Chapter 16

- *What are the reasons that Van Helsing gives to take Mina to the castle?*
- *Who travels with Quincey?*

Chapter 17

- *What happens on the hilltop?*
- *Why does Van Helsing remove the hinges of the doors?*

Chapter 18

- *What do Van Helsing and Mina see from the hilltop?*
- *How does Dracula die?*

Chapter 19

- *What happens to Arthur, Seward, Jonathan and Mina after seven years?*
- *What are Van Helsing's final thoughts?*